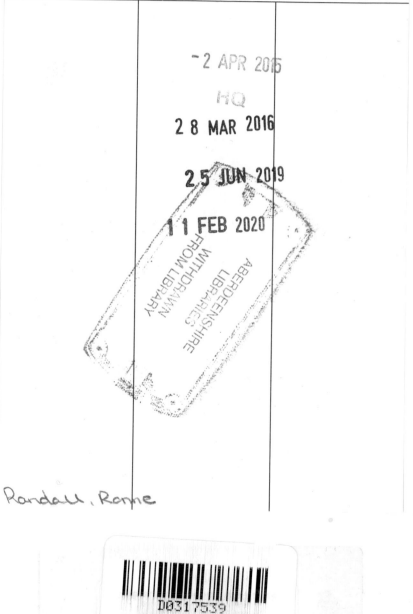

Note to parents, carers and teachers

Read it yourself is a series of modern stories, favourite characters and traditional tales written in a simple way for children who are learning to read. The books can be read independently or as part of a guided reading session.

Each book is carefully structured to include many high-frequency words vital for first reading. The sentences on each page are supported closely by pictures to help with understanding, and to offer lively details to talk about.

The books are graded into four levels that progressively introduce wider vocabulary and longer stories as a reader's ability and confidence grows.

Ideas for use

- Ask how your child would like to approach reading at this stage. Would he prefer to hear you read the story first, or would he like to read the story to you and see how he gets on?

- Help him to sound out any words he does not know.

- Developing readers can be concentrating so hard on the words that they sometimes don't fully grasp the meaning of what they're reading. Answering the puzzle questions on pages 46 and 47 will help with understanding.

For more information and advice on Read it yourself and book banding, visit **www.ladybird.com/readityourself**

Book Band 8

Level 3 is ideal for children who are developing reading confidence and stamina, and who are eager to read longer stories with a wider vocabulary.

Special features:

Detailed pictures for added interest and discussion

Wider vocabulary, reinforced through repetition

Once there was a boy called Tom. His big brother Will was a knight, and one day Tom wanted to be a knight just like him.

Longer sentences

When he grew up, Tom became a squire for an old knight. He helped the knight look after his armour, his lances and his horse.

Simple story structure

JS

Educational Consultant: Geraldine Taylor
Book Banding Consultant: Kate Ruttle

A catalogue record for this book is available from the British Library

Published by Ladybird Books Ltd
80 Strand, London, WC2R 0RL
A Penguin Company

001

© LADYBIRD BOOKS LTD MMXIII
This edition produced for The Book People Ltd MMXIV.

Ladybird, Read It Yourself and the Ladybird Logo are registered or
unregistered trademarks of Ladybird Books Limited.

ISBN: 978-0-7232-9369-9

Printed in China

The Red Knight

Written by Ronne Randall
Illustrated by Emma McCann

Once there was a boy called Tom. His big brother Will was a knight, and one day Tom wanted to be a knight just like him.

One day, Will had to go far away.
He gave Tom a golden coin.
"Keep this," he said. "I have one
just like it."

Tom did not see Will again.
He missed his big brother.

When he grew up, Tom became a squire for an old knight. He helped the knight look after his armour, his lances and his horse.

But when the old knight died, there was no one for Tom to look after. He missed being a squire, but he helped look after the horses at the castle.

Tom liked looking after the horses, but he still wanted to be a knight some day like his brother.

One day, a noble knight in red armour came to the castle. Many people came out to look at him.

"Who are you?" asked the people.

"I am the Red Knight," said the noble knight. "Who will joust with me?"

"I will joust with you," said a knight. "My squire here will help me with my armour and lance."

"I do not have a squire," said the Red Knight. "Is there a boy here who can help me?"

"I can help you," said Tom. "I was a squire once, and I can be your squire now."

Tom helped the noble knight with his lance and he helped him with his armour.

Many people came to see the joust.

The knights took up their lances
and their horses ran at one another.

Suddenly, the Red Knight's lance broke! Tom ran to get him a new lance right away.

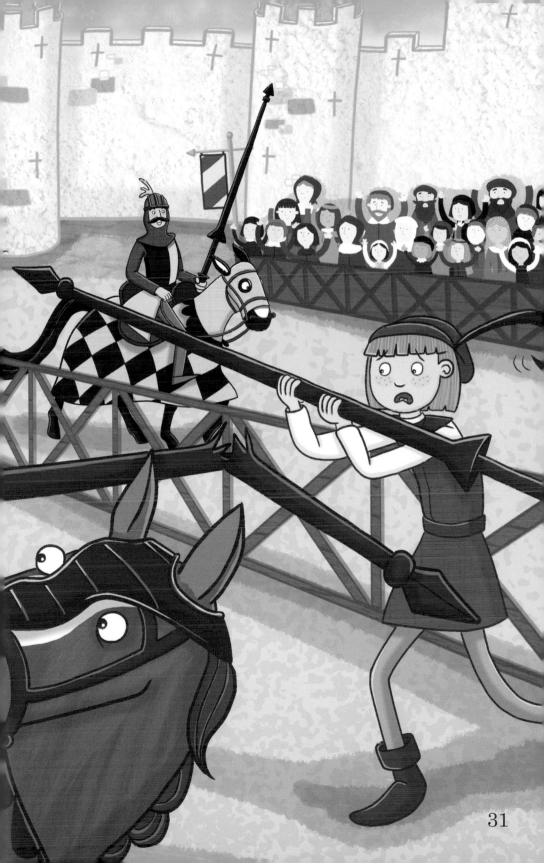

The Red Knight won the joust!
"Hooray for the Red Knight!"
called all the people.

"You were a big help to me," said the Red Knight to Tom. That made Tom happy.

Tom helped the Red Knight
with his horse.

He helped the Red Knight
take off his armour.

Suddenly, Tom saw that the
Red Knight had a golden coin.
It was just like Tom's own coin!

"My brother gave me a golden coin!" said Tom. "You have the same coin. Are you Will, my big brother?" he asked.

"Yes, Tom, I am your brother," said the Red Knight.

"Will you be my squire again?"
Will asked.

"Yes!" said Tom.

43

Tom was very happy to be with his big brother again. And he was also happy that one day he would be a noble knight, just like Will.

How much do you remember about the story of The Red Knight? Answer these questions and find out!

- What is the name of Tom's big brother?

- What does Will give Tom to keep?

- What does Tom do after Will leaves?

- What does the Red Knight break during the joust?

- How does Tom know the Red Knight is his brother?

Look at the different story sentences and match them to the people who said them.

"I will joust with you."

"I was a squire once, and I can be your squire now."

"Hooray for the Red Knight!"

"You were a big help to me."

Read it yourself with Ladybird

Tick the books you've read!

For more confident readers who can read simple stories with help.

Level 3

 YOU won't like this present as much as I DO!

 The Elves and the Shoemaker

☐

☐

 Hansel and Gretel

 Harry and the Bucketful of Dinosaurs

 Jack and the Beanstalk

 Furi on Music Island

 Poppet Stows Away

 Rapunzel

 The Red Knight

☐

☐

☐

☐

☐

☐

☐

Longer stories for more independent, fluent readers.

Level 4

 I am Inventing an INVENTION

Harry and the Dinosaurs United

☐

☐

Heidi · Katsuma and the Art Thief · Luvli and the Glump-a-tron · The Pied Piper of Hamelin · Sam and the Robots · Snow White and the Seven Dwarfs · The Wizard of Oz

☐   ☐   ☐   ☐   ☐   ☐   ☐